Mindscapes

G. O. Clark

Mindscapes
By G. O. Clark

All rights reserved. No part of this book may be reproduced or transmitted in any form or by any means, electronic or mechanical, including photocopying or recording or by any information storage and retrieval systems, without expressed written consent of the author and/or artists.

Mindscapes is a work of fiction. Names, characters, places, and incidents are products of the author's imagination. Any resemblance to actual events or persons, living or dead, is entirely coincidental.

Poem copyrights owned by Gary O. Clark
Cover illustration "Mindscapes" and cover design by Marcia A. Borell

First Printing
May 2024

Hiraeth Publishing
P.O. Box 1248
Tularosa, NM 88352
e-mail: hiraethsubs@yahoo.com

Visit www.hiraethsffh.com for online science fiction, fantasy, horror, scifaiku, and more. Stop by our online bookstore for novels, magazines, anthologies, and collections. Support the small, independent press and your First Amendment rights.

Introduction

When putting together this collection of speculative poetry, I was trying to decide how to create a cohesive table of contents. Should I group the poems by subject matter, length, alphabetically by title; what I considered the best poems up front? After an hour or so of ceiling gazing consideration, I put aside the rules for literary success, and put the poems in chronological order, by final copy date; April 26, 2019 to April 11, 2023. It seemed logical.

The collection within these pages is a stroll through roughly four years of my poetic meanderings, chasing many of the same tropes I have in the past, and visiting unexplored territory when the spirit so moved me. With Spring in the air, it was time for a poetic weeding of my aging mind; "Mindscapes", for lack of a better title.

There's no guided tour. Be sure to exit through the gift shop at the end, remember where you parked, and, thank you for your attention.

G. O. Clark

Contents

Gravity
The Return
A Night Of Melting Symmetry
Reluctantly Joining The 21st Century
The Servants Of Reality
Boots
What Once Was Pitch Black
Nuclear Winter's End
The Aroma Of Other Worlds
Connected By Clouds
Two Oceans
Crop Circles Explained
Snowflakes
Beresheet Fail
Old Toys
Floating City Blues
Clues
I Am Providence
Heat Wave
Diva
A Week In The Life Of
Haunted Black Holes
Conspiracy Theories
Waiting
Held Over Indefinitely
Class Songs Mashups
Einstein's Eyes
Eagle
The Martians
1968
WW III
Magnifications
A Clear View Of The Future

Three Hearts As One
Junkmail
Memorial Day
The Evening News
The Wall Of The Universe
A Message From Above

Dedicated to granddaughter Lilly.

Gravity

It stays
marble angels
from taking wing

while keeping
old man moon at a
gentlemanly distance.

The Return

Everything
depends upon the
old silver rocket

buffeted
about by the harsh
Martian winds,

so distant
from the warmth
of the Sun.

A Night Of Melting Symmetry

Phosphorescent snails slither
forward over the driveways and
sidewalks of our sleepy little town,
their glittery trails imprinting
the secrets of the insect world for
those savvy enough to translate the
obscure poetry of tank treads.

Overhead, space clowns
are arcing across the night sky,
their clown shoes propelling them
like underwater flippers,
their big red noses all lit up
to warn off approaching aircraft.

At the all-night Donut Palace,
two off-duty cops sip coffee and
share the highlights of their day on
an old blackboard, white chalk
piercing the calm like a stuck siren;
clock behind the counter, melting.

We sleepers are confined
inside our human limitations,
our dreams using the props at hand to
flesh out shooting scripts of the mind,
our darkened bedrooms turning into
landscapes peopled by melting
symmetries and irrationality.

Reluctantly Joining The 21st Century

They all have smart phones,
I Phones, plastic, soft cornered
rectangles of instant information
and two-way communication;

I have an old flip phone capable
of two-way, one-on-one conversation.

We're all cells in a great
network of microwaves, watched
over by satellites, each of us a single
atom in the e-tower of Babel;

the SF paraphernalia of the past
comfortably warm in one's pocket.

Assimilation is a given, my
attention to reality about to lose focus,
the screen's glow ready to draw me in
like the bug to a Zapper.

The Servants of Reality

A formation of silver saucers
hovers over the Capital Building
in D.C., but nobody notices,
much to busy to stop.

Three witches chant above
their caldron in the Jefferson
Memorial, but nobody notices,
much to busy to stop.

King Kong clings to the top
of the Washington Monument,
awaiting recognition, but nobody
notices, much to busy to stop.

The Lock Ness Monster
does laps in the Reflecting Pool,
but nobody notices, much to
busy to stop.

A Unicorn nibbles the green,
green grass of the White House
lawn, but nobody notices, much
to busy to stop.

The presence of the fantastic
is obscured by the blinders of
bureaucracy, wonders ignored,
too myopic to notice.

Boots

A boot has been found
on Mars, size 14, once white
but now covered with a layer
of Martian dust; faded insignia
on boot shaft not of human origin.

Speculations as to its
owner abound; a stranded
astronaut from Earth's future,
or piece of debris from a wrecked
space craft of alien design?

In the years to come, as we
explore the Martian landscape
step by step, footprints marking
our progress, the other boot may
finally turn up, answer snug within.

What Once Was Pitch Black

The light outside of galaxies,
is soothing to distant travelers
on their journey to find new worlds;
the Sun just another star riding
the ripples of memory

Nuclear Winter's End

In stark sunlight,
scattered about the
cold winter tarmac,
frost covered acorns
glisten like tiny
glass eggs,

black crows high
above, fast-frozen in
ancient nests, their sharp
beaks stuffed into icy
breast feathers; one
thaw too late.

The Aroma Of Other Worlds

With each sip
of crème diluted coffee,
a liquid swirl transforms
into a surreal mythical beast,
a coastal outline, or vague
map of some imaginary world,
the French roast's fragrant steam
floating above each image
like translucent clouds

Connected By Clouds

It's a cloudy day on Mars,
wispy thin ones like those in the
California sky above me.

Above its surface, water ice
clings to red dust particles; Earth,
O2 N2 functionality

It looks like another drought
year coming, Mars burning bright
in the cloudless night sky.

Two Oceans

At the sea's edge,
pieces of flotsam and jetsam
strewn along a receding trail of
fresh laid footprints, and the sun
sinking with all the heaviness
of another world.

Come darkness the stars
burn bright above the salty mist,
moon but a sliver, distant, invisible
planets hiding in their orbits like
mythical sea creatures in
the ocean's depths.

Walking the beach
between these two oceans,
ghost's of explorers past whisper
encouragement, etch maps in the sand
with bony fingers, their compasses
pointing straight up.

Someday we will step foot
on more distant shores, debris
from earlier attempts in our wake,
boots etching tracks in virgin sand;
then, as now, wanderers poised at
the tide lines of two oceans.

Crop Circles Explained

Crop circles,
the result of momentary
landings

of future Earth vehicles,
their varied anti-grav engine
signatures sometimes

simple, sometimes intricate,
patterns in those farm fields an
unintentional side affect,

time travel a fickle thing,
though advanced enough to
avoid man-made structures;

no Amazon vans from
the future crashing through
a customer's roof.

Transformation

Snowflakes
are angels who
have departed Heaven,
their crystalline souls
frozen for a few brief
moments in the body
of a Winter storm,
before becoming
grounded.

Beresheet Fail

Earthly tardigrades
now residing on the Moon,
vacuum secure.

[Wikipedia:
https://en.wikipedia.org/wiki/Beresheet]

Old Toys

Toy Rotary Phone

Always had a smile,
unreal friends at other end,
faceless texting now.

Pogo Stick

More downs than ups,
stick repurposed in garden,
boy no kangaroo.

Barbie & Ken

For Barbie and Ken
it was true love at first sight,
the end of their line

Toy Gun

A toy six-shooter
safe in evidence locker,
cop on paid leave

Toy Piano

Hunched over the keys,
audience still quarantined,
fresh torture begins

Minefield

The Legos robot
turns into a minefield,
after lights out.

Floating City Blues

The new Tower of Babel is
located in the Cloud.

It's not the floating city
of science fiction novels and films.

It's an unlimited gigabite obelisk
stuffed with noisy content;

Information, information,
information, information overload!

I've got them floating city blues,
trapped inside the hive-mind.

Clues

A hollowed out moonlet
spinning between the orbits
of Mercury and Venus.

Two sets of footprints,
following a well worn path on
the dark side of the moon.

Frozen bones beneath
the ice caps of Mars, silently
awaiting reassembly.

Metallic debris scattered
among the rings of Saturn, one
with the ice and rock.

If only Uranus, Neptune
and Pluto, could talk, what tales
of visitation they might relate

when our probes cruise
within their orbits, generations
after the fact.

Our own back yard is full
of clues cry many, while we still
focus on distant stars.

I Am Providence

The wind is strong,
the wind chimes silent.
A wind from nowhere, its
duration determined by the
clock without hands.

It bodes well, it bodes
ill. It swells the ragged sails
of the swimming pool boats
abandoned in the back yards
of suburban ghost towns.

According to myth,
the nowhere wind is older
than mankind, an established
phenomenon preceding the
coming of the elder gods..

The TV weather maps
are all frozen in time, no
meteorologists left to state the
obvious, cloned news anchors
hiding off camera.

In Swan Point cemetery,
Lovecraft's tombstone plays
host to fading whispers, memorial
flowers turned to ash; ultimate
gate flung wide open.

Heat Wave

So hot
the blue sky has
faded,

to off-gray.

The roses
on the vine have turned
to potpourri,

caught in breezeless limbo.

And the squirrels
are draped over the elm
tree limbs,

like tiny,
Daliesque fur coats.

Diva

The diva has taken total control of
the moment, even up here in the ninth
balcony, voice ringing clear on every level,
high notes and low ranging equally from
the audible to the telepathic,

base notes rattling the spine like a
a sub-woofer in some ancient low riders
Chevrolet, treble notes piercing inner and outer
ear with all the subtlety of a blow torch
heated ice pick, her performance

staged against the backdrop of
a spiral galaxy, her angelic voice lingering in
the mind long after her bow, along with the image
of her quivering voice tubes, more mesmerizing
than any Earthly Medusa's hair.

Haunted Black Holes

The ghosts
of previous universes
haunt our present one,
cosmic microwave
detected, haunting
black holes and
knocking the classic
Big Bang theory
off its shelf.

"based on theory by physicist Roger Pentrose
and others", Live Science online.

Conspiracy Theories

The planets
are just humongous
balloons, but Earth is
real, and party
central.

The Moon, all
moons, are hollow
and house various alien
species who consider us
their pets.

The Sun is
actually Hell, Satan
its eternal landlord, rentals
always available; no
WiFi or cable.

These are just
a few, confined to our
immediate neighborhood,
the non-lizard people
believe true.

Meanwhile, back
in reality, a secret group
of blue-eyed men control
the world, openly meeting
on golf courses.

Waiting For The Real

Bare blue Winter sky.
Slight gusts of wind unable to shape
any clouds into things childhood
familiar or mythic.

I'm waiting here for something to happen.

I understand when I watch the action
on TV, behind the varied images are random
pixels, toneless static, electronic noise and
cosmic whispering.

I'm waiting for something, anything, to happen.

Take away the computer generated
imagery, the action sequences of alien crafts,
indestructible actors, and car chase acrobatics,
and just a blue screen remains.

I'm waiting for something real to happen.

The sun on my back is slipping
into shadow, the sky still empty blue.
Gazing skyward, I wait for a movie to begin,
for something, anything, real.

Held Over Indefinitely

Within the bombed out city,
surrounded on all sides by the
brick and mortar rubble of lives
once spent in everyday routines,
and the metal and rubber corpses
of the wheeled American dream,

the old art deco movie theater
still stands, seemingly untouched
by the alien rain of midnight death,
their fiery projectiles, each with an
untranslatable hieroglyphic greeting,
like WW II bombs in the past,

its movie theater marquee
silently stating in bold red letters,
H. G. Wells' War Of The Worlds,
In Color by Technicolor, limited
engagement, bargain matinees daily;
snack bar popcorn machine still
full of moldy, green death.

Classic Songs Mashups

Tiny Tim

Godzilla
tip toeing through the
tulips.

The Police

Bug eyed monster
peering into the young
cheerleader's room.

Hendrix

A hazy sky,
screams and sirens, the
crayons are melting.

The Doors

Detroit, Halloween
night, setting the night
on fire, again.

Michael Jackson

Dark city night,
rain soaked alleyway,
Jack rippin' it up.

James Taylor

Rosemary peering
into her baby carriage
for the first time.

Bob Dylan

Sentient boulders
attacking a bus load
of desert campers.

Simon & Garfunkel

Brooklyn Bridge,
East River below teeming
with alligators.

Rolling Stones

Lando's cloud city
under attack by Imperial
storm troopers.

Elvis

Cujo reincarnated
as a fat basset hound,
with killer instincts.

Led Zeppelin

Dark stairway
in football stadium,
straight to Hell.

Grateful Dead

Band members
turning skeletal while
performing top 10 hit.

[see back pages for song titles]

Einstein's Eyes

What did you see in them, Dr. Abrams?
When Albert was still alive, you kept your
distance, treated those eyes professionally,
prescribed the needed lens corrections. But
after he died, what possessed you to remove
them; spirit them away from the autopsy.

Did you see yourself reflected in them,
the self you wished you could have been,
an icon recognizable the world over? Or
staring into that glass jar of lifeless white
and brown orbs, did you glimpse the past?
The future? The actuality of the present?

Perhaps you had visions of looking through
them like the lens's of H.G.Wells' Martians,
see our kind through alien eyes. Some believe
old Albert *was* an alien. Is that your secret?
After microscopic examination, did you find
telltale signs of something not of Earth?

Or maybe you just wanted to hold them
every so often, gaze into them, and make a
brief connection to his past brilliance. Become
privy to the secret of his intelligence, at one
with his neural processes; a clone of his genius,
not merely a high IQ voyeur.

Then again, maybe you wanted to be part
of the myth surrounding Albert, his eyes as
collectable as a Babe Ruth autographed baseball,
a lock of Marilyn Monroe's hair, or JFK's top hat.
A unique souvenir to pull from hiding and share
with dinner guests, drinks all around, the story
you solemnly relate stranger than fiction.

It seems a bit macabre you hanging onto Albert's eyes all these years. Not for so-called experimental reasons like Dr. Harvey, old Albert's brain in a labeled formaldehyde filled jar. I guess you had a reason. Was it curiosity? Fifteen minutes of fame? The pursuit of scientific truth?

Then again, perhaps you had no reason other than just not wanting to let him go. Staring deeply into those eyes, mesmerized from the very first, your emotions transcended your intellect and as with the ashes of a loved one, you couldn't let him go. Time and space being what they are, we'll probably never know; the eyes still locked away.

The Eagle Has Landed

My cat stares at the old news footage
of Neil Armstrong as he giant-steps down
upon the surface of the moon.

To her feline sensitivity, he's just a big
silver feathered bird, not unlike those others
perched in our tree, this event just a

slight diversion from her usual evening
routine of eating, catnapping, and clawing the
furniture; television a curiosity, the moon
a poor stand-in for the warm sun.

The Martians

Ingenuity
records proof of life on Mars,
old NASA parachute.

1968

Mushroom cloud poster
replaced by the Whole Earth one,
future malleable.

WW III

Where have all
the sunflowers gone?

Nuclear winter, say scientists.

Old expiration dates
on sun screen reflect the
beginning of the end.

The end times a real spoiler.

Things electronic now
a thing of the past, dialog a
post-humanity relic.

The birds no longer tweet.

Military actions have
replaced war, the new definition
of enemy, all inclusive.

Missiles whistle death's song.

English gardens have
withered, while royal portraits
rot within their frames.

Death only exempts the buried.

Where have all the
sunflowers gone.

Magnifications

Van Leeuwenhoek
looking in, Galileo looking
out, the micro and
the macro;

a sea of animalcules,
in a water droplet, and the
banded patterns of
muscle fibers;

the ocean of the night,
dotted with pure light scattered
as if by random by the hand
of some unseen god,

and the massive Moon,
its detailed imperfection evident
for the first time to Galileo"s
inquisitive eyes.

Each man of science
looking to magnify nature,
to magnify the mysteries
of reality.

A Clear Vision Of The Future

The explorer's eyes
are rheumy,
weakened by old age,

yet the bright light
of the infinite
still shines through,

galaxies, stars, planets
and moons,
cosmic wonder,
labeled by association

out there
beyond the telescope's
sealed lens, silently
awaiting

the clear eyes
and beating hearts
of young explorers,
curiosity primed

by ancient maps
penned by old men
with rheumy eyes,

comfortably cradled
in their easy chairs
of gravity.

Three Hearts As One

The rancher gazes
out the bedroom window
at their backyard,

autumn lingering
in the trees, patio chairs
rusting in place,

dried up bird bath
abandoned long ago by her
favorite songbirds.

Behind the rose bush,
decades old roots nourished
by her alien ashes,

the salvaged piece
of silver fuselage fashioned
into a headstone;

Her Two Hearts
Beat As One For
Too Brief A Time,

the simple epitaph,
their secret secure within
his single heart.

Junkmail

Another day
of my mailbox being
stuffed with junk mail,
thanks to someone selling
my name and address to
to a nonprofit list.

This morning
there were pleas for
donations to the Native
American, generation
starship creation and
relocation fund,

plus a glossy
pamphlet from the
questionable, Endangered
Alien Species Relief Group,
representing aliens affected
by racial injustice and
human diseases.

And let's not forget
the Society Of Homeless
Spirits, those unlucky dead
trapped in limbo between
Heaven and Hell, their
sad souls bound up in
eternal red tape.

These are but
a few examples of the
junk mail clutter received,
which I know I could avoid
if I did everything online,
with the help an email
spam folder.

But I'm a writer,
old fashioned, and like the
feel of paper in my hands, the
occasional responses to my
creative endeavors, like
contributor copies and
signed checks.

People tell me to
join the 21st century, to
quit living in the twentieth;
it's 2035, for God's sake man!
Whatever. The electric whine
of the postal van calls to me
each day, hope alive, trash
incinerator primed.

Memorial Day

They're reading the names of the dead,
nearby at the town cemetery, followed by
a sole bugle player performing Taps, this
carried on the breeze to my back patio.

The dead of three world wars, Korea,
Viet Nam, Iraq and Afghanistan; World
War III the latest between us and the
aliens, fought to a stalemate,

no one the winner, forces regrouping here,
and out there. Their home base has yet to be
determined by our military; the distances
too vast, early warnings spotty at best.

Sipping my cold morning coffee,
the occasional odor of burnt out buildings
and death lingers in my memory, a direct
opposite of 4th of July fireworks.

A bird's eye view from above my
house and the surrounding neighborhood
would show destruction far and near, with
a few patches that escaped the chaos.

A lucky few survived the brutality;
a street here, mobile home park there, the
town cemetery, the aliens imprecise targeting
not unlike that of a tornado.

The cemetery is filling up, the list of
names getting longer each year, the aliens
still out there somewhere, just waiting for
the right moment to exterminate us, plant
their flag, and declare a holiday.

The Evening News

Science fiction
has now become the
evening news,

1950's rockets
going up, then coming
down to land upon
their tails,

autonomous
EVs pulled over
by cops, owners napping
in the back seat,

miracles of medicine
broadcast nearly every
month, disease on the run,
life spans inching up,

the future getting
brighter with each click
of the remote, in between
all the commercials.

The Wall Of The Universe

Far into the future
we come upon the wall of the universe,
its top and bottom stretching out of sight and mind,
the material of its construction mysterious
      and black
as the inside of a rumored cave deep within Earth,
where no light from any sun has ever shined.

What waits beyond the wall
is not for human eyes or fragile psyches,
the true unknown better left to the safety of fiction
and song, to evenings round a cozy fire,
      drinks in hand,
one's imagination left to run wild
      while safely confined
within the boundaries of fact and logic;
      new equations
waiting behind the wall, beyond our blackboards.

There's those who say
the true meaning of existence lies on the
wall's opposite side, that all our philosophical
quandaries will be answered, laws of physics not
presently known categorically illuminated;
      the unified
field theory finally coalesce and become textbook
      accepted.
Or perhaps there's nothing waiting there
      but a vacuum
where the old gods hibernate, and new gods
      gestate.

The wall of the universe
is timeless, its shrouded mysteries eternal.
When I cease to exist, consciousness slipping
into pure nothingness , I'll leave language behind
on the tongue-tips of future explorers who
challenge
the wall's infinite barrier, seeking answers
to this existential ambiguity of life.

A Message From Above

The UFO
is your friend, embrace it.

Hug it close
in the memory of your arms.

Swallow it
like a lozenge in the mouth
of your mind.

Celebrate it
in song and rhyme, and I Believe
poster art.

Join hands with your
chosen brothers and sisters,
within the crop circle.

Keep the faith,
as they will come to take the
blessed above,

into the night sky,
where gods hide and ghosts
enjoy eternal WiFi.

Classic Songs Mashup titles.:

1. Tip Toe Through the Tulips
2. Every Breath You Take
3. Purple Haze
4. Light My Fire
5. Thriller
6. Sweet Baby James
7. Like A Rolling Stone
8. Bridge Over Troubled Water
9. Get Off Of My Cloud
10. Hound Dog
11. Stairway To Heaven
12. Touch Of Grey

Acknowledgments:

"The Return", *Analog Magazine*, Nov/Dec. 2020.
"Servants of Reality", *Cosmic Horror Magazine*, #12, 2021.
"Boots", *Utopian Science Fiction*, Vol. 2:1, August/Sept. 2020.
"What Once Was Pitch Black", *Analog Magazine*, Jan/Feb. 2022.
"The Aroma Of Other Worlds", *The Martian Wave*, November 2022.
"Two Oceans", *Illumen*, Winter 2022.
"Crop Circles Explained", *Illumen*, Winter 2022.
"I Am Providence", *Lovecraftiana*, (GB), 2023.
"A Week In The Life Of", *JOURN-E*, Vol. 2, No. 1, 2023.
"Einstein's Eyes", *Einstein's Eyes*, Dreams & Nightmares, #123, 2023.
"1968", *Martian Wave*, November 2022.
"Three Hearts As One", *Asimov's Science Fiction*, May/June 2023.

G. O. Clark's writing has been published in *Asimov's, Analog, Space & Time, Midnight Under The Big Top, Daily SF, HWA Poetry Showcase VII* and many other publications over the last 30 years. He's the author of 16 poetry collections, the most recent, "Tombstones: Selected Horror Poems", 2022, Weird House Press. His third fiction collection, "Aliens & Others", came out in 2021 From Hiraeth Publishing. He won the Asimov's Readers Award for poetry in 2001, and was Stoker Award finalist in 2011. He's retired, and lives in Davis, CA. http://goclarkpoet.weebly.com

Books & Chapbooks by G. O. Clark

Letting the Eye to Wonder (1990)
7 degrees of something (1991)
A Box Full of Alien Skies (2001)
The Other Side of the Lens (2003)
Bone Sprockets (2004)
25 Cent Rocket Ship to the Stars (2007)
Mortician's Tea (2009)
Strange Vegetables (2009)
Shroud of Night (2011)
The Saucer Under My Bed and Other Stories (2011)
White Shift (2012)
Scenes Along the Zombie Highway (2013)
Gravediggers' Dance (2014)
Twists & Turns (2016)
Built To Serve: Robot Poems (2017)
The Comfort Of Screams (2018)
Easy Travel To The Stars (2020)
Aliens & Others (2021)
Tombstones: Selected Horror Poems (2022)

www.ingramcontent.com/pod-product-compliance
Lightning Source LLC
LaVergne TN
LVHW041639070526
838199LV00052B/3455